J

2015

OCT

# The Pied Piper
## and the
# Wrong Song

Written by Laura North

Illustrated by Scoular Anderson

## Crabtree Publishing Company

**www.crabtreebooks.com**

**Crabtree Publishing Company**
www.crabtreebooks.com
1-800-387-7650

616 Welland Ave.
St. Catharines, ON
L2M 5V6

PMB 59051, 350 Fifth Ave.
59th Floor,
New York, NY 10118

Published by Crabtree Publishing in 2015

To Dylan — L.N.

**Series editor:** Melanie Palmer
**Editor:** Kathy Middleton
**Proofreader:** Shannon Welbourn
**Notes to adults:** Reagan Miller
**Series advisor:** Catherine Glavina
**Series designer:** Peter Scoulding
**Production coordinator and**
**Prepress technician:** Margaret Amy Salter
**Print coordinator:** Katherine Berti

Text © Laura North 2013
Illustrations © Scoular Anderson 2013

First published in 2013
by Franklin Watts
(A division of Hachette
Children's Books)

Printed in
Canada/022015/IH20141209

**Library and Archives Canada**
**Cataloguing in Publication**

North, Laura, author
       The Pied Piper and the wrong song / written
by Laura North ; illustrated by Scoular Anderson.

(Tadpoles: fairytale twists)
First published 2013 by Franklin Watts.
Issued in print and electronic formats.
ISBN 978-0-7787-1934-2 (bound).--
ISBN 978-0-7787-1960-1 (pbk.).--
ISBN 978-1-4271-7698-1 (pdf).--
ISBN 978-1-4271-7690-5 (html)

       I. Anderson, Scoular, illustrator II. Title. III.
Series: Tadpoles. Fairytale twists

PZ7.N815Pi 2015      j823'.92      C2014-907779-3
                                                          C2014-907780-7

**Library of Congress**
**Cataloging-in-Publication Data**

CIP available at Library of Congress

This story is based on the traditional fairy tale,
The Pied Piper of Hamelin, but with a new twist.
Can you make up your own twist for the story?

In the town of Hamelin,

there were rats everywhere.

"The Pied Piper can help us,"
said the mayor.
"He plays a magic pipe that
makes the rats go away."

So the Pied Piper arrived in town.
"I will get rid of your rats!"
he promised.

"If you can do that," said the mayor, "I will give you ten bags of gold."

"No problem," said the Pied Piper.
He took out his magic pipe and
started to play.

The rats looked up at the Pied
Piper. Not one of them moved.

But one by one, all the cows in the town started to follow the Pied Piper's magic song.

"Oh no!" said the mayor.

"What are you doing?"

"I don't know what went wrong!"
said the Pied Piper. "Let me
try again."

This time all the pigs began to follow the Pied Piper, dancing in a line to his tune.

"Come back!" the mayor shouted to the pigs. "There goes all our bacon!"

14

"Oh dear," said the Pied Piper.

"This doesn't usually happen."

"Let me try again," said the Pied Piper. He started to play.

All the farmers started to dance along merrily, heading for the hills.

The farmers left their gates open,
and their farm animals escaped!

The goats were eating the flowers.

The pigs were sitting in armchairs.

And the cows got into bed.

One clever boy named Peter had an idea. "Take these," he said, giving everyone earmuffs.

"You won't be able to hear anything that the Pied Piper plays."

The Pied Piper said, "I know I've got it right this time!"

He played his magic pipe.

But nobody moved at all.

24

No one heard a thing.

Not one rat, cow, pig, or farmer.

And the rats were still everywhere!
The mayor gave up. But the people
of the town paid the Pied Piper
—to go away!

# Puzzle 1

Put these pictures in the correct order. Which
event do you think is the most important?
Now try writing the story in your own words

30

# Puzzle 2

Choose the correct speech bubbles for each character. Can you think of any others? Turn the page to find the answers for both pages.

# Notes for adults

**TADPOLES: Fairytale Twists** are engaging, imaginative stories designed for early fluent readers. The books may also be used for read-alouds or shared reading with young children.

**TADPOLES: Fairytale Twists** are humorous stories with a unique twist on traditional fairy tales. Each story can be compared to the original fairy tale, or appreciated on its own. Fairy tales are a key type of literary text found in the Common Core State Standards.

**THE FOLLOWING PROMPTS BEFORE, DURING, AND AFTER READING SUPPORT LITERACY SKILL DEVELOPMENT AND CAN ENRICH SHARED READING EXPERIENCES:**

1. **Before Reading**: Do a picture walk through the book, previewing the illustrations. Ask the reader to predict what will happen in the story. For example, ask the reader what he or she thinks the twist in the story will be.

2. **During Reading**: Encourage the reader to use context clues and illustrations to determine the meaning of unknown words or phrases.

3. **During Reading**: Have the reader stop midway through the book to revisit his or her predictions. Does the reader wish to change his or her predictions based on what they have read so far?

4. **During and After Reading**: Encourage the reader to make different connections:
   **Text-to-Text**: How is this story similar to/different from other stories you have read?
   **Text-to-World**: How are events in this story similar to/different from things that happen in the real world?
   **Text-to-Self**: Does a character or event in this story remind you of anything in your own life?

5. **After Reading**: Encourage the child to reread the story and to retell it using his or her own words. Invite the child to use the illustrations as a guide.

**HERE ARE OTHER TITLES FROM TADPOLES: FAIRYTALE TWISTS FOR YOU TO ENJOY:**

| | | |
|---|---|---|
| *Cinderella's Big Foot* | 978-0-7787-0440-9 RLB | 978-0-7787-0448-5 PB |
| *Hansel and Gretel and the Green Witch* | 978-0-7787-1928-1 RLB | 978-0-7787-1954-0 PB |
| *Jack and the Bean Pie* | 978-0-7787-0441-6 RLB | 978-0-7787-0449-2 PB |
| *Little Bad Riding Hood* | 978-0-7787-0442-3 RLB | 978-0-7787-0450-8 PB |
| *Princess Frog* | 978-0-7787-0443-0 RLB | 978-0-7787-0452-2 PB |
| *Rapunzel and the Prince of Pop* | 978-0-7787-1929-8 RLB | 978-0-7787-1955-7 PB |
| *Rumpled Stilton Skin* | 978-0-7787-1930-4 RLB | 978-0-7787-1956-4 PB |
| *Sleeping Beauty—100 Years Later* | 978-0-7787-0444-7 RLB | 978-0-7787-0479-9 PB |
| *Snow White Sees the Light* | 978-0-7787-1931-1 RLB | 978-0-7787-1957-1 PB |
| *The Elves and the Trendy Shoes* | 978-0-7787-1932-8 RLB | 978-0-7787-1958-8 PB |
| *The Emperor's New Uniform* | 978-0-7787-1933-5 RLB | 978-0-7787-1959-5 PB |
| *The Lovely Duckling* | 978-0-7787-0445-4 RLB | 978-0-7787-0480-5 PB |
| *The Princess and the Frozen Peas* | 978-0-7787-0446-1 RLB | 978-0-7787-0481-2 PB |
| *The Three Frilly Goats Fluff* | 978-0-7787-1935-9 RLB | 978-0-7787-1961-8 PB |
| *The Three Little Pigs and the New Neighbor* | 978-0-7787-0447-8 RLB | 978-0-7787-0482-9 PB |

**VISIT WWW.CRABTREEBOOKS.COM FOR OTHER CRABTREE BOOKS.**

# Answers
## Puzzle 1
The correct order is: 1c, 2e, 3f, 4b, 5a, 6d
## Puzzle 2
The Pied Piper: 1, 3, 6
The mayor: 2, 4, 5